CW00859926

Tales of Tara

The Awakening

A Novel Inspired by a True Story

Tara Shen

Cover Graphics/Art Credit: Matt Joffe

Balboa Press books may be ordered through booksellers or by contacting:

Balboa Press
A Division of Hay House
1663 Liberty Drive
Bloomington, IN 47403
www.balboapress.com
1 (877) 407-4847

Print information available on the last page.

ISBN: 978-1-9822-2140-9 (sc)
ISBN: 978-1-9822-2139-3 (hc)
ISBN: 978-1-9822-2141-6 (e)

Library of Congress Control Number: 2019901330

Balboa Press rev. date: 04/11/2019

Contents

Acknowledgements

This book would not have been possible without the guidance of Archangel Gabriel, the communicator, who watches over artists and writers.

I am truly grateful for all of my healers, guides and mentors.

I would like to thank Raven Dodd for her editing services and helping me bring this book to its final manuscript. Raven truly preserves the authors' voice.

I am also thankful to Rita Bittner for her editing help in the early phases of the manuscript.

"To heal the body you must first heal the mind"

Chapter One

A New Nanny for Heather and Gabe

I felt the warm salty air against my skin as I walked past the sea wall that protected the land and buildings from the crashing waves of the ocean on the other side. The summer of 1991 was coming to a close. Chills ran down my spine and large goose bumps swept across my forearms. I questioned myself silently "What was that about? I tried to convince myself that this mysterious reaction was not related to the job interview that was to begin in fifteen minutes or so. My experience and education were beyond the job qualifications required for this part time position. Although, I admit my confidence was a little shaky because of the stress I was feeling.

The beach club was quiet. I stood at the bottom of the stairs and looked up to the business office. Upon reaching the top of the stairs, I was cheerfully welcomed by the office manager and directed to the interview in the office of the controller. At the end of the forty minute conversation, I expressly asked the controller for the job. He informed me that he had two more candidates scheduled for the interviews the following day and I would be notified by the end of the week.

On the drive home, in the warm golden dusk many thoughts swirled in my mind. I thought about the divorce and the risk of more violence and wondered if it would be another evening of threatening phone calls. I felt time pressure, needing to get back to relieve the babysitter.

As the evening evolved from twilight, a surrealistic wave accompanied an internal roller coaster of fear, pain, and repulsion. Tired of the turmoil, I acknowledged to myself that living on the edge, walking on eggshells, and living with lies and violence had taken its toll on me.

Taking a deep breath and a gentle sign, I prepared myself to reunite with my children. Heather and Gabe smiled when I stepped into the doorway of the living room.

Twenty-three women responded to the classified advertisement I had placed in the local newspaper. Hiring a new nanny was a priority. I considered only women with excellent qualifications. The screening and interview process included her observing the candidate meeting and interacting with Heather and Gabe. Actually, only one met with the children. I made my decision.

Jessica, a very bright, energetic, warm, caring sensitive teenager, who quite obviously loved children accepted the offer for the position. Very quickly, Jessica became part of the family. The children were laughing and pulling Jessica's arm saying "let's go outside." I felt a sense of relief that the children responded this way and connected so well with Jessica. In spite of the pending divorce and my mother's progressing cancer, there radiated an atmosphere of joy and laughter.

Reaching out for help was the best choice. My mom

called me weak for finding a therapist to work with during this difficult time. I had weekly conversations with my sister Liz regarding our mother's progressing cancer no longer in remission. She was deteriorating quickly. Sadly, it seemed enviable since our mother never really changed her lifestyle continuing to use toxic substances. Denial is a powerful force in those who are addicted.

Emotional turmoil dominated much of my day to day life with my husband out of control – the drinking was obvious but there was something else going on. Something simmered under the surface, maybe some gambling I thought. The first time I time I entered the support group I felt scared and extremely angry as well. I did not have too many people in my life to give me support, guidance and understanding. Considering what was going on in my house, the response from my family was minimal. As I gained greater understanding of myself, I realized there was hope. The therapist and group members were warm and communicated directly and honestly and created a safe place.

I felt tremendous chaos at this time both internally and externally. The thought that I had almost sole responsibility for my two young children overwhelmed me at times. The children were affected by the instability and the outbursts.

When the police officer brought my husband, Jason, to the house to pick up some of his personal belongings, I could feel my heart pounding in fear. He collected a few items of clothing and another box of miscellaneous items I had packed for him, so that he would not have to stay longer to gather them. As he was leaving, he raised his right hand, pointed his index finger in my direction and with a mean and harsh tone he threatened, "I'm not going to give you a f---ing dime". The police officer escorted him down the stairs. The phone calls were to resume later, they were pretty much always the same "LIFT the F---ING RESTRAINING ORDER" in the usual bullying tone.

At their young ages of four and two, this was s confusing for Heather and Gabe. I certainly did my best to keep them away from situations that would be disturbing to them. At least some of the neighbors knew somewhat of what was going on. They certainly had seen the police cars or maybe heard some of the noise.

The evening would wind down after dinner, and playing outside with the children was a relief from the stress. All the problems seem to have started at the beginning of the previous year. I had found a book at the town library, "You Can Heal Your Life" by Louise Hay and another book "Healing the Child Within" by Charles Whitfield, MD. I devoured them. They opened a door for a major transformation in my life. This is exactly what I needed.

CHAPTER TWO

Anger: The Backbone of Healing

I felt sadness about the impending divorce, even though I knew it was the right choice. The turmoil, verbal abuse, violence and chaos made our home life intolerable. Jason and I made several attempts to save our relationship with the help of a psychiatrist who had worked with us for about six months over a year ago. Dr. Brent had been recommended to me by a friend. Even after several interventions Jason could not stop drinking. Dr. Brent clarified the truth very simply "alcohol has a pretty good hold on Jason". Another intervention I arranged was Jason's company's employee assistance program. They did a formal evaluation. Jason later admitted to lying on a few questions. Finally, I hired an independent intervention specialist to coordinate a formal intervention with several key people in Jason's life. This specialist advised me that after assessing the people closet to Jason, that it was not likely that an intervention of this kind would be effective. After these efforts, I made the decision to leave, to move forward and not look back.

Every other weekend I drove with Heather and Gabe an hour and a half way to my mother house to help out. The house looked much the same as it did when I lived there, which was most of my childhood and college years. The trees in the front yard were taller and fuller and there was now central air conditioning. My mother was mostly bed ridden now and on oxygen. A tall oxygen tank stood on the side of the bed. The values on the top of the tank were almost as high as the headboard. My mother's arm was swollen almost double its normal size. On her chest was an X mark several inches long and wide, a leftover target for the radiation therapy. While there for the weekend, I would make meals, do laundry, and manage the mail and on alternate weekends my brother would do the same. During the week, a dear friend of my Mom would spend the day with her, and their was also hired LPNs to see that she had meals and the medical issues such as medications were taken care of.

One warm summer afternoon I met with a prospective divorce attorney that had been recommended by my therapist, that I had been seeing for several weeks. Janet Weston, Esq. recently achieved publicity through winning a landmark case. Attorney Weston represented a defendant, who had been tried for second degree murder. The woman defendant had assaulted her husband after years of him inflicting domestic violence, battering and cruelty on her. The court found the defendant not guilty and dismissed it as self-defense.

I found the little white house that had been converted into an office. The waiting area had white walls, dark wood furniture and a simple floral framed print on the wall opposite the brown leather couch I sat on while flipping through *People* magazine. Attorney Weston entered, standing about five foot six with shoulder length ash blonde hair and slightly bobbed and wearing a hunter green tailored dress that was knee length. Ms. Weston motioned with her hand for me to join her in the main office suite. I stepped in cautiously into the room and sat down in one of the chairs facing the large desk in the center of the room. I nervously looked around at the books, file cabinets, and dark furniture. I explained to Ms. Weston that my husband had been frequently violent at home which lead me to obtain a restraining order, she interrupted me and asked if I had a copy of the order with me. After placing the document on the desk facing Attorney Weston I explained that I had gotten a temporary restraining order about a year and a half ago. My tone, posture and facial expression exuded anger and rage. Although it felt appropriate to me, my harsh speech, frowning, and redness of my face and the ringing of my hands reinforced this. Attorney Weston pointed out these gestures to me and suggested quite firmly that I work on my anger before proceeding with the divorce. She specifically recommended a program for codependency and adult children of alcoholics' intensive program. I thanked Ms. Weston for her time and gathered my things and papers and walked through the waiting room to my car outside the door. A few tears flowed down my cheeks, I wiped my face with my hand. I noted the warmth, apparently from the anger.

My therapist that had referred me to the attorney was quite familiar with the program suggested and she had several clients that had positive participation in this intensive program. The therapist and I contacted the admissions, the referral was made and my insurance information was provided. Planning began immediately, I wanted the nanny to stay with the children while I was gone. My awareness of the synchronicity that was taking place became quite clear. Everything seemed to be falling into place. The surfacing anger erupted and with it came fear and a sense of urgency. In taking care of the practical things, I purchased groceries and washed, folded and organized clothing for Heather and Gabe. I packed my own clothing and other necessary items. I felt very confident in Jessica's ability to care for the children in my absence. I gave Gabe and Heather each a long warm hug. I drove off in my navy Ford wagon feeling hopeful that this program would be beneficial to me. The two-hour drive seemed much shorter than that. I located the building where I needed to check in. I parked the car and climbed the five stone steps to the main entrance to the facility. The counselors were welcoming and smiled when greeting me. In a large central room, I met the others to be in my group. After finding our rooms that were assigned to us, we all gathered in a large living room.

That evening, we started working as a group. I noticed that the group members were well educated professionals. There were two counselors assigned to this group of eight individuals, one male, Steven and one female, Marcy. The common factor of the group members was they were all adult children of alcoholics and were having problems with codependent relationships and compulsive behaviors. Steven and Marcy began right away with ice breaker exercises and games and quite quickly the group members began to feel comfortable. I felt safe in this group setting. The level of intimacy exceeded anything I had experienced before. Group members were sharing intimate details of abuse from there families of origin. Now, they had an opportunity to tell the truth and express their real feelings, instead of stuffing them.

In the group on the second day, I created a family sculpture psychodrama that was from an actual incident from when I was six years old. I selected different group members to act as real persons at the scene. I instructed the group members to re-enact an event when I was playing outside with my sister and some neighbors. I was wearing a pink cotton dress that had ties in the back and delicate embroidery on the front. As I was running, my sister was behind me on a bicycle actually chasing me, the front wheel of the bike hit the back of my shoe and then it went up my leg. As I was describing the scene to the group members they attentively played their roles. I felt a burning sensation and I reached back to my leg and looked down at my hand and there was blood.

At this point, my sister lost control of the bike and headed over the handle bars. I ran up the front yard. Within seconds, my sister Liz opened the front door. Blood was gushing from her chin. Our mother gasped and raised her hand over her mouth to cover her facial expression. Liz looked into the large mirror on the wall in the living room behind the piano, her chin bone could be seen through the wide cut. Our mother asked what happened, Liz shouted "Tara pushed me." 'Immediately, my mother grabbed me by the arm and pulled me down the hall and began slapping my bottom and right on the scrape on the back of her leg. The scene of the family sculpture concluded, the two counselors facilitating the group looked at each other, one of them stated in a firm clear voice: "There was a lot of abuse going on here" 'Having created a simulated re-creation of a piece from my early life, I felt the truth had been observed and validated by safe supporting others. This therapeutic experience was quite powerful and it allowed participants to integrate and transform themselves at the core of their being.

In this process, each participant had an opportunity to express their buried pain and anger in the presence of caring witnesses. As the week progressed, the level of intimacy among members of the group increased. Healing bonds were formed. There was the experience of joy and laughter which had additional therapeutic effects. The group became united. Steven and Marcy, as primary counselors in this group experience, reminded participants that this 5-day experience was like psycho-surgery, so to speak, meaning that buried emotional wounds have been uncovered and it would likely continue to emerge from the unconscious minds, therefore aftercare was essential. Each group member met individually with a counselor to collaborate and design an aftercare plan that was appropriate to their specific needs.

I reviewed my aftercare plan with my primary counselor, which included group and individual therapy and some twelve-step work. In recalling my experience for the week, I felt confident and supported and I was reminded that the counselor told me to pay attention to my arms. At the end of the family sculpture, after releasing some anger I noticed and shared with those present that I felt tightness around my arms just above my elbows. Following the aftercare plan review, I joined the others in the lounge area. Everyone was sharing numbers and addresses to stay in contact.

Some of the group members commented that I seemed to have gone through the most dramatic transformation. After hugs, tears and good-byes, we all drove off while waving honking and promising to get together soon. The ride back through the mountains of Pennsylvania went smoothly. Having released so much anger and tears, I felt lighter. I was looking forward to seeing my children, it had been five days. On the passenger seat next to me was the little book I had purchased "Affirmations for the Inner Child". It contained daily meditations and affirmations as well. I was very pleased with my purchase, something for me to turn to in difficult moments. I also had phone numbers of everyone in the group to reach out to if I needed to.

The children and the nanny were waiting on my return and were very happy to see me, especially since now my warmth towards my children was enhanced because I was more centered and relaxed after the healing work I had done.

Chapter Three

Managing Memories and Perspective

I returned to the weekly routine of dealing with my mother's physical decline as her cancer progressed, the pending divorce with the final restraining order still in effect, the job search and preparing my daughter Heather to begin kindergarten. I also needed to be mindful of my aftercare plan which included group therapy weekly, alanon meetings and regular individual therapy appointments. My son, Gabe, was still in diapers. I was running a small consulting business, which I moved from the dining room of our townhouse, to the loft space of one of my clients office. With all of this happening the last thing I needed was stalking, harassment, and terroristic threats.

Well, sure enough, the counselor at the intensive program was right. There was definitely something going on with my arms- there's a saying in recovery that "the body remembers what the mind forgets". My arms were remembering something really big. There was the intensity of the fear, terror and anger. I now knew that there was something in my past that was sexual. I needed to connect on the phone with my sponsor from the alanon program. My sponsor had identified some of my symptoms as those associated with incest. I knew members of my group therapy were working on their issues and the aftereffects of incest. I felt disgust when hearing them describe these experiences. Boundary violations were common in family systems with alcoholism. Sometimes, an offender would drink to make it feel okay to act out sexually.

In another regular session with my group. I felt particularly overwhelmed with rage and feeling a sense of doom. My therapist suggested I try releasing some of this with the Bataka bat. I knelt down facing the foot rest, which was regularly used for this purpose. I grabbed the handle of the bat raised the bat over my head and pounded down with the bat on the foot rest as hard as I could. My therapist suggested that I begin directing my anger and verbalizing my thoughts. I yelled "I hate you", I hate you……and my therapist asked "for what?" with one last exhausting pounding with the bat I yelled "for holding me down" I bent over toward the floor and began sobbing. The therapist said "this trauma had been waiting to come out for a really long time." I felt a little dazed and sat back down in my chair. I calmed down a little and began taking a few deep breaths and listened and waited until the end of the session. By the time I got home I was almost sleepy and felt a little sense of relief. There was laundry to finish, dinner to prepare, mail to read and phone calls to return, and time to play with Heather and Gabe. It was the end of another challenging day.

Jason continued to call, usually in the evening, even though there was a final restraining order in place. It was a court order stating that neither party could contact the other, no communication or contact what-so-ever was allowed. This did not matter to Jason, besides, he was a risk taker. He would use his usual bullying and intimidating tone demanding that I lift the restraining order. I felt confused sometimes because I knew that he had moved on and was seeing someone else and someone new. I learned from the programs that the alcoholic needs someone to lean on, because if they are still active they can't stand on their own.

In the months leading up to the separation, I had noticed there was definitely some problem gambling. The money was a big issue. I wanted to move through the divorce process as quickly as possible. The stress was continuous and tremendous, thinking back to the time, I spent at the intensive program when all I had to concern myself with was working on my recovery, no work, no housework, no housework, no children, no running around doing errands. It was almost the weekend and time to pack up the car and the kids and drive an hour and a half to my mother's home. (It had been my home for decades, many memories). I found dealing with my mother more difficult now. She would blurt out random comments, at times, that seem to validate the memories I was having. One afternoon, while helping my mother cleaning to bathroom and my mother abruptly said "you deserve a metal". I made a note of it and brought it back to my therapy group.

These every other weekend visits were somewhat boring for the children. My mother's home had a beautiful and good size backyard, but there were not many toys. I would bring a brunch with me as well as books and art supplies. My mother was bed ridden now, with a large oxygen tank next to her bed. Even after her cancer surgery, chemo and radiation, she had never quit smoking. I began to realize that now my mother was getting closer to her final days and now finally, it was becoming safe to remember.

I had been involved in alanon for about a year now. The way I interacted with my mother had changed, because I learned to detach from verbal assaults and abusive comments to some degree and I also cultivated the courage to stand up to her in a nonconfrontational manner. The concern for my children was ever present, as they could not help but be exposed to some of the harsh comments by their grandmother towards me. Being mindful of the fact that this was subsequent to the exposure to their father's verbally abusive comments and witnessing him throwing things at me. I observed the reflection of the damage this had by the sadness and confusion in my daughter's facial expressions.

The past year or so seemed like a blur. Just the summer before, on a family reunion on the Island of Nantucket, was beautiful, peaceful, and scenic. Warm summer breezes blowing on the quiet sandy beaches, the family experienced relaxation and joy. Myself, Jason, Heather, Gabe, Lz, Liz's husband Jack, and daughter Kelly, my brother Ray, his wife Nancy, and their town children Margaret and Robby gathered in a large home not far from the beach, Some of the family dynamics were strange and awkward, as the group sat having dinner before sunset.

Liz, as the oldest, took the leadership role. She resembled the family 'hero'. Liz initiated various activities for the group to engage in for fun. I jokingly asked her if she was the cruise director. In my recovery, I gained more awareness, now the dysfunction was obvious. Everyone played the part of the looking good family and particularly tried to maintain polite and appropriate discussions and activities in front of the children. This was the last summer reunion in which the drama and trauma remained in the unconscious memory- everything was about to change.

Chapter Four

Remembering the Trauma

I sat for a few moments in the kitchen at the table having completed the laundry. It had been a long day, as I glanced at the clock, I observed 11:11. It was late I needed to get some sleep. The next morning, in the awareness of ever present fear and terror I knew some of it was surfacing from the past, some of it was very real in the present. One day at a time, I would remind myself. I felt the danger potential of my husband persisted, he drank and gambled and was a also a batterer. I had also reached out for support from family since we were so vulnerable. After all, they were there for the wedding, the baptisms, birthdays and other holidays, I really needed them now.

The good thing was now he was dating someone and that kept him distracted and gave him less time to harass, stalk and make terrorists threats.

After having been on several interviews, I felt discouraged. Fortunately, I still had my small business going and it continued to generate some revenue. All in God's time, I thought. I still attended weekly group and individual therapy sessions. I knew I had been hurt sexually and physically in the past and I was feeling much more panic and anxiety. My sponsor was in the process of forming an incest group and they had selected a facilitator. I repeatedly asked to join the group. I had to wait, because the members needed to invite me in. Impatience and urgency overwhelmed me. I felt nauseous at times.

The weekend arrived, time to go and help my mother. I really did not want to go. My mother had a long history of being hypercritical. And now was no exception. I spoke with my sister Liz on the phone weekly. She often provided validation of some of the dysfunction we both experience growing up. I previously shared with her that I was having memories of sexual abuse, Liz talked fearfully and timidly about a neighbor across the street who had done the same to her. I knew from her tone that it was real and still affecting her today.

I bought a copy of "Courage to Heal" by Ellen Bass and Laura Davis, which at the time was the bible how to get through the aftermath of sexual abuse. At this point, I was in the crisis stage was rushes of emotions, periods of exhaustion, flashes of pieces of memories, sometimes pictures- a scene from the past, a face or there would be smells maybe a whiff of scotch or a sensation in the body.

I was dependent on my therapist, my group and others recovering from their childhood pain. Money was tight now that my husband was required to pay me only $225 per week for child support. It was awarded me by the court with the final retraining order. In all likelihood, that amount would not change until the time of the divorce. The financial situation added to the uncertainty and contributed to an increased sense of panic and impending doom. I continued my therapy and healing journey in spite of financial stress. In a conversation with my sister Liz I explained my journey.

"I've gone this far, I know I can't stop and I can't go back, I need to keep moving forward toward the whole truth"

Liz was the family hero, she excelled at everything, academics, athletics, music, theater, leadership roles and social activities. This excellence was the family expectation. Each individual was expected to get top grades, achieve excellence in every area of life and demonstrate perfect behavior, these great expectations for the family system that valued looking good above all else. It was imperative, so no one would see what was really going on. Unfortunately for me, this visade worked.

As I pushed forward with my process, the pain and the confusion seemed to increase at times. Jason's harassing phone calls were consistent and predictable, even so they were extremely upsetting producing fear and panic. I knew that batterers usually follow through on their threats. Not complying with the restrictions of the restraining order was now the accepted norm.

It became necessary for me to rely on Jessica more often. Finally, I got the news that I would be permitted to join the group for survivors of sexual abuse. It would begin in January. Diane was the new babysitter I found to fill in when Jessica was playing soccer or occupied with other activities. When it did not feel safe at home I would bring Heather and Gabe to Diane's house up the street.

A feeling of desperation set in, I really need the new group to start. Meanwhile, I found another group that addressed the issue, it was a twelve-step program. Going the first time felt scary. Marcie, a fellow survivor from my regular group offered to go with me to give me support. The two of us sat in the large room in a corner near the door. In this meeting there were twenty or more people, men and women, shaking and fearful, I wondered how so many could have experienced these horrible acts. I felt terrible. As my, sinuses swelled and throbbed, dizziness and nausea overwhelmed my body, I listened to others sharing pieces of their stories.

The format for this meeting included each person introducing themselves by the first name an stating that they were a survivor and named the perpetrator by their relationship to him/her or them. Some survivors at the meeting did not know who, because that information had not come forth yet. For me it was a terrible evening- who would want to be here- everyone was present because they had to be. We had to walk through the pain.

Now, I was dealing with a new layer of anger- that I needed to go to these meetings. This was not how I envisioned my life to be. I was missing out. Where this journey was taking me was unknown. So, what was it that kept me going? A little bit of faith in the process that I learned to believe in, beginning in April 1990. That time was only a few weeks after the first restraining order. Yes, it was faith in the process, belief that life would get better when the truth was revealed.

There were also signs of a spiritual nature. For example, meaningful coincidences, events that were synchronistic were happening. It could be that a universal spiritual power was in charge. I noticed 11:11 on the clock again.

Watching the children play in the backyard, I knew I wanted to protect them from harm. I felt confused about who was safe and who was not. I received a phone call from my cousin Mitch. He was calling about his Aunt, my mother. This phone call triggered a surge of panic and anger. I was angry at my cousin and I was not sure why.

After making a simple chicken, rice and vegetable dinner, I was aware that preparing food that the children enjoyed and tasted good to them was important, in contrast to meals that were disgusting from my childhood. Nurturance and nutrition can go together to make healthy eating a pleasurable experience.

After dinner they played for a little while and read a book together. I did not feel well. I prepared a bath for the children and went into the adjoining bedroom to lie down for a few minutes. I had a gush of panic, my heart started pounding. I began my breathing that I had been taught in therapy and my reading as part of grounding and coping skills. Heather and Gabe were already climbing into the tub. I found 2 cans of shaving cream in the linen closet and gave one to each child. The children were having a ball, laughing and splashing. In the next room, I was lying down my body was shaking uncontrollably, at this point I picked up the phone and called a supportive fellow survivor. The fear and panic escalated into felling of terror- the memory became clearer. My cousin was holding me down, my uncle ripped off my bathing suit and then I gasped, I could see the summer sky the light blue twilight with creamy, orange, wispy feathery clouds through the window. My legs were shaking and for a moment I returned to 1991 in my room I could hear my children laughing and splashing again. The support person on the phone explained that she thought I should go to the hospital…I yelled “NO” “I won’t” I remembered what my therapist had said

“your husband could use this against you.”

Finally, I felt the rape, it was my grandfather. I went numb, this memory had been trying to get out for months. The voice at the other end of the phone kept telling me that I was going to be alright.

“if you survived it before you can certainly survive it now”

I kept breathing and praying. I brought myself back to the present. The children were done with their bath and settled down to watch their favorite movie “Beethoven”. It occurred to me that the children would perceive my state of upset, and I checked my calendar for my next therapy appointment.

The surfacing of these memories changed my perceptions of multiple situations and issues. I felt exhausted and I slept through the night. I had a much better understanding now of my memories when I explained this to my sister. Liz had been preparing and making plans to come east to stay at our mother's. I felt like I was on an emotional roller coaster, from rage, to sadness, to panic and then followed by confusion. I thought it would never end. I now had three therapists one for individual therapy, another for group therapy, and a third for the special group for sexual abuse. My individual therapist attempted to comfort me by saying:

"we hope we are over the worst."

A wisp of relief was a welcomed experience, now it started to make sense. Several whys were answered by the recall of the events of many years. Complimentary reading answered other unknowns. Traumatic events repressed are acted out or acted in. Much of life's weirdness had been explained. I felt better with a big piece of the puzzle filled in.

CHAPTER FIVE

A Significant Ending

I answered the phone on the third ring, "hello"

"Hi, Tara, it's Liz, just got here this morning…

"Umm, okay"

"when I was at the hospital Mom's friends were visiting her. They were talking about the old days, and saying how much fun she was, you know, laughing and joking"

"really" I replied

"Is this the same woman who was our mother, I was thinking" Liz revealed. We both laughed.

I thought back to last spring when, the progression of the cancer was made known and Liz suggested pacing ourselves because it could be a long haul, and sometimes it's hard to gauge.

Over the next several weeks, Liz and I had nightly phone calls, usually when Liz returned home from the hospital. It gave us both a chance to process old and new feelings about our mother.

The memories continued to come forth, over the next weeks more of the pieces about that day…that horrible day. I found drawing my feelings and memories helpful. It also made it more real, without that acceptance of the truth I would easily slip back into denial. I had been told by one of my therapists that it took a lot of energy to hold down those memories. I was releasing the memory, there would be more energy.

The memories had been frozen in time and when they melted they were quite intact. Many details were well preserved. The emotions had been frozen as well, so when they finally came forth, liquefied they were big and powerful. Over time I learned a repetitive sequence of my process- as follows: the body sensation, the emotions and finally the visual, the pictures of what had happened. If there were specific smells associated with the memory it would be experienced somewhere between the body sensation and the emotions.

More about that fateful day was surfacing I felt myself standing at the top of the stairs, feeling dizzy and I raised my arms to gain balance to no avail I fell forward down the stairs, at the bottom of the stairs I hit my head on the wall straight ahead. I could hear conversations going on in the next room. This fact was disturbing, why weren't they helping me. There was blood everywhere and going down the stairs someone wrapped me in sheets, they were full of blood as well. The throbbing pain pulled me into a less conscious state, my head ached and throbbed with pain. I could hear conversations in the kitchen. I panicked that they didn't seem concerned about me. Shock, terror, pain, overwhelmed me. Someone made a phone call to a pediatrician.

I scheduled another therapy appointment. A flood of memories with emotion overwhelmed me. I also needed to process some guilty feelings of needing to withdraw from the situation with my mother. I did in fact talk to my sister every evening usually around 9 or 9:30 in the evening. The spiritual path I was on kept me feeling as though I was being guided through all of this. Everything was happening for a reason. The truth was rising to the surface in perfect timing.

Liz phoned "It would probably be a good idea to start getting ready, we have an appointment with the social worker at the hospital to discuss and make arrangements for discharge planning". The appointment was scheduled for 9 AM on the 28th of February. I bought new shoes for Heather and packed clothes for a few days for myself and the children. This time I didn't bring the nanny with me. That cold February morning was at least sunny. My thoughts wandered randomly from crisis to crisis. The memories, the aftereffects of the abuse, my mother, the children's wellbeing with all this going on and thinking how tired I felt with this drive and the divorce and the court date set for April 6, 1992, weighed on me. I felt fear and panic, it was only six weeks away.

We reached the street where I lived starting at the age of ten. The landscape had changed over the years, the trees had grown taller and it seemed quieter without children in the street running, laughing and playing, echoed of years past. The pond where I enjoyed thousands of hours swimming, fishing, ice skating and rafting with my friends glistened in cold stillness of a cload covered February afternoon. My uncle was walking down the driveway, as I pulled the car in front of the house just passed the mailbox. As I stepped out of the car and unbuckled the carseats for the children, my uncle walked towards me and said

"I am sorry.. your mother passed early this morning" and he gave me a hug.

He helped me carry the suitcase in, as I assisted the children. On entering the house, a wave of emotions of both grief and relief came over me at the same time. Liz sat in the kitchen at the table and was talking on the phone, she stopped for a moment to says hi.

The phone rang non-stop for several hours. As arrangements were being made for the funeral and the wake. Liz had taken over the responsibility for making those calls. Our mom had selected cremation. I looked at the clock, it read 11:11, I spaced out for a moment. Liz and I worked together to make arrangements, making phone calls to friends and family. We also planned a luncheon after the funeral service. My children played with their cousins. Once again there was laughter in the house.

Old family friends seemed to come out of the woodwork, people Liz and I hadn't seen in a decade or longer. I remembered that Erica, the healer, had said it would be like my life was passing before my eyes. I answered a phone call from one neighbor who now lived in North Carolina, he was the son of my mother's best friend. He said his father had passed away.

His father was the person my sister indicated to me

had sexually abused her. I recalled the same man (our neighbor at the time) watching my sister and I in the bathtub. Friends and family called and gathered over the next several days. At the end of the day after the funeral, I thought about how I knew the things that had happened so long ago. I believed my mother blocked it out of her mind, consciously that is. How could she just go on-living a regular life knowing that this had happened. I would never be able to have that conversation that would answer these questions that were ever present in my mind.

The funeral mass ensued on a cold gray March morning. My son, now two and a half, wore the red sweater his grandmother had knitted for him. St. Theresa's church bells echoed through the corners of the cathedral ceiling. Liz read the eulogy, that she had stayed up half the night writing. It sounded frivolous and simple reminiscent of the little things our mother use to do, like The New York Times crossword puzzle. I guessed it was more appropriate than reminiscent of the memories I was having. I felt deep inside – this was bullshit. I was all about getting to the truth.

After the church service many went to the memorial center that our mom had requested her ashes be kept. Cremation was a first for the family that had always had a cemetery burial. Sadness over whelmed me with the realization that too many questions would not be answered. I started to pack up the kids stuff and was deciding when I would begin the drive back. I said some more good-byes to friends and family.

Chapter Six

The Divorce

It was 1992, an election year, George Bush was finishing up his term in office. I put the kids juice back in the refrigerator and on the door was a magnet holding an announcement to the Green Evan Alumni Association meeting at the Woodland Club. I thought, ah ha, another clue. My mother, in general, communicated very indirectly, it was always a guessing game. I believe in God's world there is no such thing as a coincidence. I knew this meeting announcement on the refrigerator had some sort of significance or special meeting, partly because it was my father's alumni association and he died 25 years ago. I saved this announcement, thinking its true meaning would surface eventually.

Well, the game was over, I moved forth on my mission to find the truth. The investigation followed. The funeral was over and I was remembering other funerals recalling the surrealistic nature of the emotional energy. The cover dissolving, as family members passed and the truth about their lives could be spoken more freely without fear. Our family was riddled with fear and most often the message was "don't you dare" [speak the truth]. Some things would never be talked about, reinforcing the denial, and repressing the truth and creating confusion and insanity with all of the unexplained aftereffects.

I made it back home, feeling tired and the fear returned. The pending divorce was only weeks away. The threatening phone calls had subsided some, but I never would know for sure when I picked up the phone whether the caller would be angry and hostile. It put me in a state of hypervigilance. I knew I needed to get back to my meetings and therapy, seeking a safe place and safe people. Two years into my intense healing process. I knew once begun there was no turning back.

At a group session, I slipped into spontaneous age regression, the triggers at my mother's funeral were taking effect. My therapist pulled me back into present day to deal with my adult responsibilities and I was reminded that my husband would use what happened to me when I was a child against me, in regard to the divorce and custody of the children.

After a couple more phone calls to my attorney, everything was set for the first week in April. On that sunny brisk morning, the wind circled around the cold stairs of stone leading up to the court room. I passed through the security and walked to lounge area with tables and chairs to meet my attorney. He explained to me again that with the signing of the divorce agreement they would be dissolving the final restraining order. I clearly was ambivalent about this in that I was still in fear of Jason. Even with the restraining order he continued stalking, harassment and terroristic threats. My attorney claimed that he did a good job for me. The agreement was relatively simple and the visitation schedule was not complicated. Practically speaking having a restraining order would make joint parenting almost impossible. The general visitation schedule included visits with their father every other weekend, the children were to be picked up by 5 PM on Friday and returned 5PM on Sunday. I felt an overwhelming numbness.

Chapter Seven

Handling Business Matters

I shared the responsibility of executrix for my mother's estate with my sister Liz. As part of this role, I was to sell my mother's home. Now the house where I had lived for many years was quiet. The painful feelings started to emerge again. The memories I had re-experienced in recent months were vivid and powerful. The remembering of the significant traumatic event explained quite a bit of why I felt the way I did…in addition it offered insight to the different choices I had made, why I avoided certain people and for example, I sometimes would refuse to go a family gathering, and I would avoid interactions with my uncle. I was afraid of men in general. I became fully aware of this fear by the time I was seventeen and asked my mother if I could see a therapist. Her response was "I have to think about it." As a young teenager, I use to work out with weights until my arms became extremely strong and I would challenge some of the boys to arms became extremely strong and I would challenge some of the boys to arm wrestling, I usually won. I was not going to be held down and raped again.

I recalled several weeks back when I re-experienced the rape.

I was flashing back…blood was all over, I could hear the voices downstairs, I felt dizzy, I took a few steps to the top of the stairs. The bleeding would not stop, and my head started spinning. My breathing was shallow, everything went black. Next, I rubbed the top of my head, I curled up on the floor in a ball. And I looked up the stairs where I had fallen from…questioning why my father didn't do anything about this. I wondered: Did he know?

About a year before my mother died. While visiting her in the hospital when she was being treated for cancer, she had trouble breathing because it was in her lungs, she seemed to be a little out of it she mumbled that Mitch (my cousin) shouted "Grampa did something terrible".

I was gasping for air feeling stunned and shocked and numb, I could hear sharp, panicky voices in the kitchen. I recalled wondering when was someone going to do something.

Back to 1992, in the master bedroom of my townhouse, I was lying down exhausted releasing all the energy of another piece of the trauma. That afternoon was almost too quiet, I made great efforts to ground myself after the memory retrieval. The content of the material that had surfaced needed time to be processed. This new information swirled in and out of other memories of a couple decades and I cried again. I needed to bring myself back to 1992, at least in my body and my mind to actively participate.

On Tuesday evening at my group therapy session. I shared the recall of the next part of that day and I held up a drawing and paused a couple of seconds in the direction of each group member asking them to bare witness to my truth.

On Tuesday evening at my group therapy session, I shared the recall of the next part of that day and I held up a drawing and paused a couple of seconds in the direction of each group member asking them to bare witness to my truth.

Liz and I worked together to get our mother's business matters in order. The medical bills and insurance was handled by Liz, she had worked as an office manager for doctors, so she was familiar with the procedures and details of the paperwork. The house was about to be put on the market and I arranged to meet with the realtor and the attorney. I arrived at my mother's house with Jessica, Heather and Gabe. Signs of spring were everywhere. I felt some sadness and peace, the reign of terror was over, or so I thought.

Maybe a calm before the storm was happening, the four of us settled in with our bags and toys. A trip to Pizza Hut was in order as there was no food in the house. Heather and Gabe were active and loud in the restaurant, Jessica chuckled and whispered to me

"are they always like this?"

"Kinda." I replied.

Back at the house, Jessica played with Heather and Gabe, while I was in the kitchen making a few phone calls, opening mail and recording bills in a ledger. The will allowed for Liz, myself and our brother Seth to divide the furniture. A company had been hired to come in to do a complete inventory of everything in the household and give each item a fair market value.

As the evening slipped away Jessica settled in one of the bedrooms. Heather and Gabe felt safer being closer to their Mom. It had been a long day, the three of us bundled together in the family room and watched one of our favorite movies. I was exhausted and drifted off to sleep on the floor wrapped in a comforter. The movie noise startled me. I reached around in the dark for the remote control, I felt both my children close to me. I sighed with the relief that the three of us were safe and they were together. The remote was found on the coffee table, I clicked it off. The room was now dark and silent. The three of us slept. The silence was broken with a thud. Something had fallen on my face, I was shocked and startled. When I touched my face I felt blood. The standing lamp had fallen over and the post portion of the lamp hit my cheek bone right below the corner of my left eye.

That panicky feeling started again. It was spooky I thought, how did it fall over. My face was sore on the cheek bone. Eventually, I fell back to sleep. It was morning before I knew it. Heather and Gabe were kicking each other, "Mom, tell him to stop." I could hear Jessica in the kitchen and decided to go in to have her take charge, so I could take a shower. I requested that Jessica take the children to the park. So that I could make some phone calls and get some paperwork done and to meet with the realtor that had been hired by my mother, to finalize the contract to put the house on the market. I was going through the mail separating the household bills from correspondence from friends and relatives. I opened the bills to check them for reasonableness and nothing seemed unusual. I made a quick call to Liz to let her know that I was at the house and that everything was okay.

The doorbell rang. I looked out through the glass window to the right of the door. Two women stood on the front porch looking across the garden in front of the house. I slowly opened the door, the women smiled and introduced themselves as agents from Wilson Peterson Realty. I welcomed them in. They toured the house rather quickly and discussed the market analysis with me. The contract was signed – the house would shortly be up for sale.

The afternoon flew by for me, my cheek still hurt and it looked red and swollen and I was exhausted as well. Jessica returned to the house with Heather and Gabe. I decided we would have some take out food tonight and not risk the children acting out and making a scene at a restaurant. The remainder of the weekend was calm. The incident of the lamp falling on my face was puzzling. I was certain that it was meaningful, after all, there are no accidents. Heather and Gabe were cooperative on the ride home, Jessica dosed off for awhile, it had been a somewhat hectic weekend. The sadness in my heart brought me to tears. The children had fallen asleep and the quietness of the evening echoed my aloneness. My marriage had ended sadly and my mother's death ended an era of deceit. In the mist of these difficulties, I experienced a spiritual sensation and I felt convinced that there was synchronicity in these events of my life. I clearly knew that many things were happening for a reason. This knowing kept me moving forward.

Chapter Eight

Finding Clues in the Family Home

The following day was difficult and the weather was getting a little warmer. I wondered if it was too soon to put on the air conditioning -sometimes I had great difficulty making simple decisions. Too much was happening at once, both internally and externally, I thought about my therapy appointment the next day, I had had little time for journaling this past week. I needed to spend time at my office, there were several things to catch up on, including a report for the attorney regarding the income and expenses of the estate over the past several weeks.

I received a phone call from someone in my group

from the intensive program, they were all trying to get together in New York City, as it marked a central location for the group. The following weekend Heather and Gabe would be going with their father. This gave me time to work on my healing, since the past several weeks I had felt a whirlwind of emotions. I checked in with Liz from time to time for validation on certain facts about the family. It helped to make everything seem real. At times, I felt that Liz was upset by these memories that I was sharing with her. Liz knew all the people and places I was remembering. With time, space, and quietness and my mother gone it was safe to remember. Each memory I recalled more and more was explained like why I did certain things. They were the key to many behaviors, choices and fears, like fear of a dark room, rough water and others. At times I felt thoroughly exhausted.

Back in group on Tuesday night "the safe place" where I felt heard, understood and believed. I listened to the ordeals that the other group members had to contend with, the empathic responses were cathartic. In turn, I shared the updates of feelings, memories, concerns about my children and everything on my mind.

When Heather and Gabe returned from visiting their father they seemed anxious and rambunctious. I suspected they may have experienced some sort of turmoil or lack of attention and possibly a good chance both.

At times, this healing work at times took its toll on me. I needed extra rest. Heather and Gabe were fighting a little since arriving back from their father's. I accepted that I had no control over what went on, it was upsetting knowing that the weekends were difficult for them as well. I put on a favorite movie and went upstairs to change the sheets on the twin beds in the children's room. I laid down for a minute when I was done. Next thing I knew, Gabe was standing in the doorway and threw a board at my face. Startled, confused and upset, this had happened before over 6 months ago, the children had witnessed Jason throwing things at me and subsequently imitated it- not so usual with domestic violence. The edge of the board was about eight inches long and two and a half inches wide. It hit me right below the corner of my left eye. Now, I was beginning to remember the next piece of what happened after the rape. I was in the car in the back seat feeling a tremendous amount of physical pain, throbbing head, terror and fear. I remember the emergency room-receiving general anesthesia-then-being awakened with a thud on my cheek. I now had a clear recall of being in a hospital bed in a hospital room it was dark and I felt the pain on my cheek. After this experience I looked forward to going to my therapy appointment. I journaled about my newly retrieved memories of more of that day. Back in group, I described what happened and made the connection of being stuck in the face (below the left eye) twice. One group member commented "you didn't get it the first time"

I also got an individual session that week….outside the therapy room someone was shuffling feet. Those sounds triggered stress reaction and feelings of panic. My therapist helped me get grounded after the brief flashback of the time I was sleeping in the hospital room and was struck in the face, I was uncertain what the object was or who was holding it, and the shuffing of the feet afterwards…the darkness of the room. Shortly after the memory and the feeling associated with it passed. I tried to figure out who it could have been. Was it someone I knew? Who else would know about this? Would I ever know? (Everything was becoming scarier.) An advantage of this process, I discovered, was the release of the negative energy and expression of the pain and the emotions associated with the memories. The intellectual integration of the historical information left me feeling clearer more centered and freer,(in less emotional stuck-ness).

The phone rang, I answered, it was the realtor with an offer on the house. I was relieved and saddened at the same time. I had been given the option to take ownership of the house as part of the settlement of the estate. The walls and stairs of the house radiated with energy of emotional and verbal abuse as well as lies, deceit and cover up, I was not sure I would get past that. With hesitancy I prepared to let go. The offer was discussed with the attorney and Liz the co-executrix. It was a cash offer and no banks were involved at all, a rather clean deal.

We accepted the offer and there was a lot of work to do between now and the closing. The entire house needed to be cleaned out. At the same time, I was trying to get copies of medical records. In cleaning the house I had found a small document from Greenford Pediatrics, with my name on it from July 1961. It had my height and weight on it, I noted how small I was. This small piece of paper (that somehow survived the decades) had the names of several pediatricians, I remembered clearly two of them. Doing my own detective work aided me focusing and encouraged me to more forward. In this process, it seems wherever I turned there were more clues and with that came validation and re-assurance that I was on a spiritual path.

Chapter Nine

Painful Memory Retrieval

Somehow, I needed to continue my healing work, with a therapist's suggestion I reconnected with Erica the healer. This woman had very special gifts and much wisdom from years of nursing. Erica's manner was very gentle and soft spoken. She worked with energy fields and could see angels. I arrived on time to Erica's home where the healing took place. I felt very safe. After the healing session we chatted for a little while and we agreed upon the date and time of the next session. Erica wrote it on a card and handed it to me.

Erica's home was a short distance from my office. After my healing session I returned to my office to complete a report for the attorney and working on the accounts of my business. At the end of the day, I picked up Heather and Gabe at their nursey school. The children sang a song on the way home, which made their ride more enjoyable. I now had a plan to spend a more extended time at my mother's home to arrange for the removal of some of the personal belongings. Quickly, I became aware of the enormity of the job ahead. I reviewed the copy of the inventory of the furnishings, paintings, actually the entire contents of the house. The house resembled a museum in ways. I decided to hire housekeepers and other helpers. The yard would continue to be maintained by the landscapers until the closing.

Jason was to be married in a couple of weeks. New concerns about the emotional reaction of the children plagued me from time to time. I considered them too young for counseling. I purchased new outfits for Heather and Gabe to wear to the wedding. The blue and white floral dress and white leather shoes fit Heather perfectly.

The two therapy groups that I was participating in were rather intense. I would share the details of the memories of the trauma I was re-experiencing, and the emotions associated with them. My process I noticed usually began with body memories, the next phase was the emotions and finally the visual (pictures in my mind of what happened). This repeated experience alerted me to the fact that repressed memories (of trauma) when retrieved, were more vivid and were in much greater detail that regular memories. In the group process, I observed that others experienced their memories differently. Some even experienced symptoms without actual memories of what happened. I knew when feelings of nausea, panic and disorientation emerged, it was likely a time that a new memory was eminent.

As time passed, I realized that a great cloud of denial and secrecy had dominated my family and community for decades, I frequently asked myself how could these things go on without any acknowledgement. As my eyes opened to the truth, more and more stories and literature exposing the facts of unthinkable abuse came to my attention. The time had come for the truth to be known.

When I observed my children, playing, laughing, running, singing and experiencing joy the question came to my mind, how could anyone take that away from a child? More physical pain through out my body seems to come out of nowhere, the emotions were sure to follow and knowing that I prepared to get the children upstairs and ready to go to sleep. I had developed an ability to mask the pain and put up a cheerful front as to not worry the children. Actually, I had been masking pain and acting as if, for years that was my primary means of survival. Acknowledging the truth that surfaced, I gasped when I realized that it actually took almost four months to remember one day. The intensity of the pain physically and the reality of what had happened, the factual material was far too devastating to process quickly, and now there were new memories to be processed, after a brief break in the process I was ready to move forward.

Heather and Gabe were with the nanny, Jessica

and her dogs, I was in the kitchen on the phone with someone from my Tuesday night group. I shared my feelings of disorientation and waves of negative emotions accompanied with overwhelming body pain. I knew I had to hang on a little longer into the evening when the children were asleep, before going further into my memories and process. The grounding and containment techniques I had been taught became useful at this time. After a few minutes I hung up the phone and two seconds later it rang again. Jessica was calling from her parents house, she explained to me that they had been watching a movie and her mother was making dinner, Heather and Gabe wanted to stay and could she bring them back in the morning?

"Okay, that might work out well." I responded.

Perfect. I thought, again synchronicity prevailed, time and space to process.

The experiences of the past several months, swirled around one more time the day of the rape from beginning to end. I looked in the mirror and could visibly see the scar under my left eye. It brought me back in time, maybe ten or fifteen years earlier when I was reviewing with my mother the times I had gone to the emergency room. We were both sitting at the kitchen table my mother was smoking, as she often was, acknowledging each incident that brought me to the emergency room, "the time you cut off the tip of your finger with scissors when you were two." My mother explained. My mother had that tone of blaming and shaming me as she reviewed each incident. She blew a big smelly puff of smoke right at me and smiling coyly in an almost hypnotic and rhythmic manner. We carefully reviewed each incident including the most recent visit, when I twisted my ankle. In remembering this time I now realized that my mother deliberately left out the visit to the emergency room after the rape. I opened up the door to the truth and now too, the extent of the coverup.

The deep pain surfaced like an enormous wave. I felt sick to my stomach and wanted to lay down to slow or stop the dizziness. I made a call to one of my group members to help me stay grounded in the present. The connection was helpful to the extent that I could hear someone on the other end reassuring me that the year was 1992.

There was an escalation of the pain and the overall sense of overwhelming fear accompanied by rage and terror. I could feel myself being carried in the darkness, there was motion moving faster, I felt myself grabbing the side of a boat, in fact I held on for dear life. I heard a deep scary voice grumbling and it came close and I was grabbed from behind, pulled back, forcing me to release the grip, that had been so tight my fingers were cramping. I gasped for breath and then felt the coldness that took my breath away completely. I was in the dark water, too scared to cry, there was some splashing the salt water tasted bad, it went up my nose and felt burning down my throat. I began screaming and choking on the water, I thought I was going to die. I suddenly returned to the present day, as usual I was exhausted. She said to focus on my breathing. My life was making more sense now.

On the way to the therapist office, I reviewed in my mind the new memories. My neck hurt, stress and pain from the body trying to process and synthesize the experiences.

Chapter Ten

Present Day Problems and Mysteries of the Past

The realization that I needed to continue my job search since the day of the divorce struck me like a slap to the head. I continued to make monthly payments for cobra, my health insurance. How was I going to be able to work at a desk and concentrate, I thought seriously, with these unpredictable flashbacks, body pain and everything else that went it. I cried in the night.

I pulled out my most recent resume from the file cabinet. I quickly scanned through the job entries. I remembered events at previous jobs that had in the past had been disturbing and with all the memories I had processed over the past several months. Those events have now taken on a whole new meaning. I needed to put all this aside as I focused on the resume, job openings and the interviews ahead.

As the past traumas were integrated, new questions came to mind about, the doctors, what did they know? And what did they do about what they knew? Was a report made? Was there an investigation? I found these plagued my mind to the point of distracting me from my day to day tasks – everything became more complicated. The simplest task could challenge me, for example making a sandwich, could be a daunting task, taking a jar of jell out of the refrigerator could confuse me. Feeling overwhelmed the memories raised more questions. To focus on anything in the moment was sometimes impossible. Where was the piece of paper I found with my mother's records? Did my mother unconsciously leave it for me to find it? I was not sure. The doctor's office address was on the paper, also the names of the pediatricians were there. Were they still alive? Would they remember? Could I find them? More information was needed. I hired a nurse to help me get copies of my medical records. I prayed that they could be found. I also made a trip to the town library. Old newspapers on microfilm could reveal some history, at least, I hoped. I selected town paper from around the time period the event occurred. I felt nauseas again almost like motion sickness. I tried to recall the pediatrician's office. One memory stuck in my mind, the rabies shots, screaming and pain. I was told that they did not complete the series as to prevent a trauma. So, they knew something about trauma. Well, it was too late the damage was done. I was now on a mission to find the truth. Current world events eluded me. My consciousness was in and out of other decades, regularly and routinely. What was happening now seemed trivial. That is accept for my children they were the upmost importance. The more I remembered the more cautious I became about being around family, who was safe, and who was not. I didn't really know for sure.

I distanced myself from almost everyone in my family some more than others, for a few reasons. One was I didn't know if they were safe and secondly the memory retrieval and healing process was regularly making me feel disconnected and freak like. Who would understand, if you had not been through it. It was difficult enough being around people that were capable of understanding and would react in a way that would not be harmful. It seemed apparent that most of the family was in denial and had repressed what had happened. I promised myself that I would forge ahead until I was healed and the truth known. The private investigation of the truth of my life continued. Sarah, the nurse helping me get copies of my medical records, listened as I explained the background of my memories of doctors and hospitals. We composed alist of names and addresses to send the releases of medical information. I tried to be hopeful of the possibility of getting further information of my real physical injuries and more details of the dates, times and procedures and treatments that were performed. As I placed my hope that the truth was out there and actually there were many witnesses, and documents and records and probably a tremendous amount of effort to cover up the truth, and possibly extensive financial cover up. Sarah volunteered her time to contact the pediatrician's office.

Two weeks later Sarah called me with some news. Sarah had found that one of the doctors in the group had, the actual date of his death was August 5, 1962, the place was Jamaica. I felt a sense of hope and excitement about the newly discovered information. At the same time, I felt fear and sadness with the realization that Dr Shane was probably only 32 or 33 years old. I wanted to know the cause of death. By this time an enormous amount of information came my way. I knew the abuse history that I was uncovering was really only the tip of the iceberg. I continued to gain courage to move forward with the support of my spiritual connection.

I spent some time researching newspapers at the library and wondering how many other people were doing the same thing, digging, searching and conducting a full investigation into the truth about their lives. Another doctor I had seen in 1971-72, a psychiatrist Dr. Berger. I vividly remembered my first visit to his office. I was having fears (wondered why?). There was a lot of secrecy and shame associated with going for psychotherapy at that time, probably because of the cover up conspiracy which was in the sub-conscious or unconscious minds of many. In the early 1970's I had several sessions with Dr. Berger at his office in Greenford. Dr. Berger lived with his family in Chester. In 1976, the newspaper revealed the story of his murder- but it was much more intriguing than that- Dr. Berger was reported to have been shot and killed by his wife, who right after shot herself. I believe now otherwise, could they both been murdered by hitmen? I felt great sadness for the traumatic loss this family experienced. The cover up is sometimes worse than the original crime. So much deceit, I was reading "People of the Lie" by F Scott Peck. The people responsible for these actins were just that. The feeling of any level of safety was now gone.

All of this new information had a powerful effect and the reality of the past kept getting darker and I started to have flashes of memories of more abuses. When will it end? I thought to myself.

Chapter Eleven

Erica the Healer

Heather started kindergarten. I chose a private school that had a full day program, Willow Tree, a small private school that offered French. At the end of the day when picking up Heather, I was in excruciating pain, a physical reaction to the triggers I encountered and my ability to focus and concentrate varied. Heather had a look of sadness about her when I walked into the school. On this afternoon, I woud be taking Heather and Gabe to a little pizza place not far from Heather's school. A wall of loneliness surrounded the core of my being. My forced smile did not fool Heather, as she fully felt my state of being.

Marcy, a good friend of Heather since the beginning of preschool had invited Heather to sleep over. I worked at acting normal when meeting with the parents of my children's friends. Heather delightfully danced with anticipation.

I used some of this feel time to journal and draw. Getting stuck in an emotion was a regular occurrence. To get unstuck I would draw the emotion. I logged a number of works of art and labeled them; 'anger', 'fear', sadness', 'terror', 'pain', etc. When the children were hoe with me I felt safer, this was due to projecting my past on the potential danger for my children. A therapist had suggested to me that they may not be safe with family members. I took this warning very seriously. The reality of these events that happened in early life made sense to me to gain an intelligent understanding on the process and knowing that I was not alone in this made a difference.

I connected and collaborated with others in the community that were organizing an event for educating and raising awareness on domestic violence and gathering resources to aid families in trouble. There was a planning meeting to host an event with members of various women's organizations in the county. I helped as much as I could, being barely out of the woods myself- during the meeting the intensity of the subject matter brought pain to my neck and spine. The feeling that I was going to get in trouble for speaking out (as I was threatened), frightened me. I knew in my heart, my soul and my mind that violence like this had to stop. A commitment to do what I could was firm and unwavering. Sometimes, people I spoke with would cringe and withdraw. Perhaps, they were still in denial of their own past or it was too much for them to fathom.

The summer was drawing to a close and I recapped the major events in the past year or so and part of that included flashbacks and memories. It took a lot of energy to hold down all those intense emotions and the repressed truth. I wanted to make another appointment with Erica for a healing session.

Erica's home was a very special healing place. Every room was like a picture in a decorating magazine and was impeccably clean. Her spirituality was reflected in the art work on the walls as well as in the beautiful vases and sculptures places on the tables and bookshelves. The colors were primarily pastels of light blue, yellows, pink and of course healing green. The rays of sunlight danced upon the soft, lush, white carpet in the room where the healing took place.

After the session, Erica offered me insight into the expected effects of the energy healing. In addition to having visual experiences of the aura energy field, Erica saw angels. I recently read an article about 11:11 phenomenon that was a gateway into a new spiritual dimensional era. I noticed 11:11 was appearing more frequently. I thought back to more than ten years previously when my lovely, compact studio apartment was in fact number 1111. I recalled on one occasion when I was walking toward the elevator; and someone mysteriously appeared, stood in front of the door to my apartment pointed to the 1111 and exclaimed poignantly "remember this number".

This particular healing session was more extraordinary than others before. Erica, an intuitive healer, had the ability to view the future. Erica revealed that she saw for me a meaningful relationship for me in the near future. She knew about the rape and name of my grandparent's maid. Erica made specific reference to hypnosis and commenting to me that I had never been hypnotized. This convinced me that she could see the past as well.

September marked the beginning of a new school year and my new position using my professional expertise. I would be working twenty-five hours per week and could be home in time to greet my children at the end of their day. I felt relieved that I could terminate my cobra health insurance. I had financial responsibility for myself and more then half of the expenses of my two children.

Chapter Twelve

The New Job

As the autumn enfolded into the beautiful colorful scenes that I once truly enjoyed, I felt bouts of fear and stress about my responsibilities. Working, taking care of my children, the pain and confusion of the grieving of my mother's passing clouded my ability to experience joy. All of the unanswered questions of what really went on in my family entered my thought periodically throughout the day. The therapy groups I participated in provided a safe place to feel my feelings and speak my truth as it was unfolding.

The emotional and physical pain that I felt from the trauma work increased the challenge in the morning.

Getting everyone out of the house in the morning proved frequently most difficult. Today my new job begins. I arrived in professional attire, fifteen minutes early and feeling a moderate amount of anxiety. With more than sufficient skills and experience to breeze through the work day for this type of position, I acknowledged that my most predominate challenge was the emotions and the aftereffects of the traumas that I continued to remember and process.

The first task of the day were the paperwork of policies and procedures and the standard employment forms. The trauma aftereffects unfortunately included sporadic moments of lack of ability to concentrate which would lead to frustration and loss of confidence. Confidence in the performance of sometimes even simple tasks was diminished. Confidence in everyday interactions with co-workers or whoever would at times feel awkward and uncomfortable for me. Could they see the abuse? I wondered.

The office space was open and had large windows,

and I had been assigned to a desk facing the window, with a calculator, a telephone and several other supply items as well. Next to my desk stood a file cabinet, a copier and fax. I was introduced to several members of the staff. After answering a few questions about my previous experience, they provided me with a project to work on that afternoon. The first task was bank reconciliations. Feeling relieved that this was not so difficult nor unfamiliar, I began working hoping that I would be able to concentrate. I soon realized that this work setting (like a few before) was a reenactment of my family of origin.

In a way, the physical setting felt like a step backwards in time. The furnishings were certainly not state-of-the-art. Ironically, the political nature of the environment placed a priority on individual rights and unions and fights over money, just like my extended family. I felt as though the conflictual energy in the office that created negativity, definitely contrary to my spiritual path. I tended, in general, to mind my own business in the work place.

Very soon in this new work position, I found it to be way below my level of experience. I discovered my post traumatic symptoms played havoc with the basic tasks at hand. Since, my concentration was slightly impaired, I needed to reread and recheck my work. What added to this was the background conversation that included derogatory remarks which started to be directed at me. It appeared to me that anyone was fair game.

Chapter Thirteen

Re-enactment in the Workplace

The evening at home included a routine of preparing dinner, playing with Heather and Gabe, a little laundry and sometimes a threatening phone call. Detaching from the content of the phone call proved to be difficult and therefore my state of mind was less peaceful.

Then not long after Heather and Gabe had fallen asleep, it started again and in more rapid progression, my memories began first in the body, then the emotions. As my body was shaking with fear I became aware I no longer was in 1992, in fact, I was back in the sixties. Barely able to sit up, I managed to journal a few words describing the images, feelings and physical pain. My sleep was intermittent that night.

Morning came. Not feeling well rested, I prepared myself for work and assisted the children as best I could. The rawness of my emotions was so pronounced. I felt others could see what happened to me, that they could see my shame. Intellectually, I knew that the shame was not mine, but the feelings needed to be processed. Opening up to the painful truth of the past injuries to the body, mind and soul, left me feeling quite vulnerable. Containment and boundaries needed to be put in place in order to meet the challenges of the day and deal with the stress created by dysfunctional co-workers, angry hurried drivers, and over-worked store clerks.

I opened up one of my spiritual books. This gave me some peace, comfort and hope that things would get better. I continued to journal my thoughts and feelings and participate in my therapy and support groups. This healing process took up a good chunk of my free time and a lot of babysitting dollars. The story of my life became clearer.

Gathering up internal strength to get on with my day, putting one foot in front of another. I got myself to work. There seemed to be some turmoil in the office and some loud voices. This negative energy vibrated against my fragile broken core.

From time to time, I needed to speak up and talk back to co-workers, that were out of line. This caused additional pressure. Offensive comments continued to accelerate. I acknowledged to myself this was not my purpose being here. I needed to work to provide for myself and my family. I felt extremely discouraged and more depressed.

Two nights a week I was attending group therapy, one for adult children of alcoholics and the other was for child sexual abuse. New pain and old pain, pushing and through the pain and then releasing. Then I reoriented myself in the present day in 1992. This process was the ultimate challenge.

One morning in the office, Victor, one of the staff, stood looking out the window noticed two women arriving at the door. They were the auditors. Victor turned to Daniel, the office manager, and exclaimed "you rape one and I'll rape the other". I was the only other person in the room at the time. I tried not to show a reaction. I was not sure what was going on. In most work places you would not get away with this. This reminded me of when years before I confronted my mother of her abuse of me and she replied "but there were no witnesses"

Unfortunately, this was not an isolated incident, yes there was more. The following week when Victor entered the office, he approached me in an arrogant manner. He held something in his hand, then held the object up to my face. Now, I could identify it. He held a ballpoint pen. The pen had a picture of a woman on it, wearing a bathing suit, and when Victor clicked it the bathing suit disappeared. There was a naked woman on the pen. Another woman was working in the office at the time, she witnessed this as well. As did the office manager, who attempted to minimize it slightly, by explaining to Victor that the action could be interpreted as sexual harassment. I spoke up and stated plainly and clearly,

"no by definition, that is sexual harassment".

Apparently, Victor felt as though he was above the rules and displayed the very same pen at another time and afterwards joked and laughed. I felt very sick. I went into the bathroom and cried. Afterall, I had been wearing a bathing suit that day I had been raped.

This was not the end of this issue. The atmosphere at work continued to be stressful and uncomfortable for me. I contacted a sexual harassment hotline, and coincidently there was a workshop coming up soon, that I received an invitation to attend and it was in my town. The social worker in charge of the hotline also informed me that there was a support group forming that would meet at a local university. I asked to be included in the group.

On the evening of the workshop, I arrived feeling

nervous and exposed. Feeling some of that shame again, I put my head down and sat down in the third row. The panel included two attorneys, a psychologist, a human resources representative and the coordinator. I estimated that there were about 30 attendees. The presentation by the psychologist was of particular interest to me, since she described the various aftereffects of sexual harassment. The effects of sexual harassment were divided into the following categories: career effects, emotional reactions, physical reactions, changes in self-perception and lastly social, interpersonal relatedness and sexual effects. I could identify with just about all of them. I felt overwhelmed and validated at the same time. This violence against women in the workplace is quite horrific in itself, so damaging and so wrong.

Chapter Fourteen

The Awakening

One afternoon, I had an opportunity to reflect back on the past months of memory retrieval. I experienced a sense of completeness. The truth had been repressed all these years began exploding into a logical continuous story. All of the weirdness and obstacles now had reasonable explanations to them. The truth will set you free is accurate, it does.

I began to feel freedom from the pain, the releasing began to quell the inner turmoil. The possibility of incipient tranquility manifested. During these lulls of calmness, I spontaneously would recall events of the past that seemed somewhat out of the norm and now assigned new meaning- reactions or re-enactment could clearly be identified.

Years of impairment in functioning in many areas of my life included relationships, academics, jobs, sleep and really everything else were explained with the surfacing and resolution of the traumas. The realization of why things were so difficult helped me let go of guilt and feeling of inadequacy.

The possibility of a better future manifested. This state of mind resulting from a spiritual practice and awakening.

About the Author

Tara Shen is a healer and an advocate of survivors of sexual abuse, sexual assault, emotional trauma and sexual harassment. As a healer, Tara supports and encourages survivors to compliment their healing journeys with various body, mind and spirit modalities such as yoga, reiki, body work and energy healing. She is a yogi and a Reiki Master.

CPSIA information can be obtained
at www.ICGtesting.com
Printed in the USA
BVHW080904170419
545788BV00013B/180/P

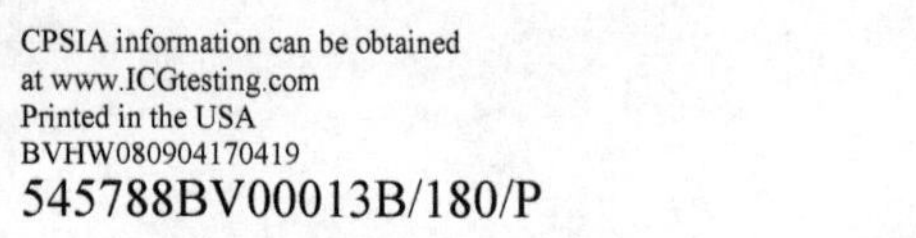

9 781982 221393